Beyond the Pages Library,

Dream your dreams, dance your dance,
& don't be afraid to take a chance!
Follow your heart!

Love,

Alex Smith

Adelyn's Dreams

Alex Lauren Smith

Fulton Books, Inc.
Meadville, PA

First originally published by Fulton Books 2019

ISBN 978-1-63338-807-9 (Paperback)
ISBN 978-1-63338-840-6 (Hardcover)
ISBN 978-1-63338-808-6 (Digital)

Printed in the United States of America

Dedicated to my niece, Adelyn Hartley. Dream big, little one, for one day you will become a woman with a vision.

1

As Mrs. Smith started her lesson for the day, she told the children, later we'll play.

Put up the crayons, the paints, and the cups.

I want to know, "What will you be when you grow up?"

All the children pondered, with loud voices they shouted:

"A nurse, a teacher, a firefighter, I'll be."

But, Adelyn just sat there quietly.

This was something for her to think about, undoubtedly.

Later that evening, while getting ready for bed,
Adelyn remembered what the teacher had said.
"Mommy, what do you want ME to grow up and be?
Because I do not know what I want to be."

"You can be anything you want to be.
You can be a pilot, a doctor, or even a mommy—like me!
You have to dream big, work hard, and never give up.
Be kind to those around you and keep your chin up!"

As Adelyn fell deep into slumber, her mind began to wonder.
She started to dream of all the things she could be—
A soccer player, a dancer, a musician she could see.

8

The score was tied, two to two,

Adelyn kicked the ball and down the field it flew.

"Adelyn, Adelyn," the crowd chanted.

She reared back and kicked it again!

"GOOOOOOAAAAAAALLLLL," the announcer roared.

The team won, she did it, she SCORED.

Look at Adelyn sporting her new white coat.

Wrapped around her neck, there's a stethoscope.

She's the best doctor for ears, nose, and throat.

She will get a few x-rays and probably tell you a joke.

When you need someone to take great care,

Adelyn, the doctor, will always be there!

12

To be on the stage hearing people scream,
She's playing the guitar, this must be a dream!
She can play the drums, the piano, and more.
Look at her fans, it's Adelyn they adore!
The sound of the bass pounding on her chest,
This feeling has set her on the greatest quest.
She wants her name on the Hollywood Boulevard Walk of fame.

Zooming through the big, blue sky,
Wow, Adelyn is soaring so high!
She is uplifted so far from the ground,
Surrounded by puffy clouds all around.
Hop aboard to fly high as a kite,
Join pilot Adelyn on her next flight.

With stage lights beaming down on her face,

Her family and friends filled the auditorium space.

The next performer up is Adelyn Hartley,

Curly haired, ballet shoes and all, with a dress so sparkly.

She twirled, she kicked, she danced,

She knew this was her big chance!

She opened her eyes and she could see,

The unstoppable dancer she could be.

"Adelyn, Adelyn, it is time to wake up.

Have you thought about what you will be when you grow up?"

Adelyn jumped out of bed and spoke with glee,

"Mommy, I dreamed so many dreams of what I could be!"

"Yes, baby, don't you see? You can be anything you want to be,
You have to just dream your dreams,
Dance your dance, and
Don't be afraid to take a chance!"

"Because no matter where you go,
No matter what you want to be,
Just remember, you will always be special to me."

As the bell rang for class,
Mrs. Smith asked Adelyn if she thought about what she will be?

Adelyn smiled, nodded, and said politely,
"There are so many things I want to be.
A soccer player, a dancer, a musician…
My mommy said it is all up to me!"

Adelyn asks, "What will you be when you grow up?"

ABOUT THE AUTHOR

Alex Lauren Smith is a graduate of the University of Central Oklahoma, where she earned a degree in Business Administration and a minor in Marketing.

With a wide range of artistic talents, Alex currently works as a men's professional clothier. She recently signed with a talent agency, where she also works as a model, actress, and promoter. In 2017, Alex was crowned Miss Oklahoma USA. During this time her mission was to encourage children to reach their fullest potential and never give up on their dreams. While pursuing this purpose, "Adelyn's Dreams" was written.

Alex plans to continue her aspirations of becoming a successful businesswoman and entrepreneur.

CPSIA information can be obtained
at www.ICGtesting.com
Printed in the USA
LVHW071915230119
605034LV00003B/17/P